Logan's Caterpillar

Sydney and Logan Series

Dianne Branch

illustrated by Kathy Kerber

AuthorHouse™
1663 Liberty Drive
Bloomington, IN 47403
www.authorhouse.com
Phone: 1-800-839-8640

First published by AuthorHouse 08/24/2011

ISBN: 978-1-4567-9952-6 (sc)

Library of Congress Control Number: 2011915353

Printed in the United States of America

Any people depicted in stock imagery provided by Thinkstock are models,
and such images are being used for illustrative purposes only.
Certain stock imagery © Thinkstock.

authorHOUSE®

To my son, Logan

One day while playing in the backyard, Logan found a caterpillar. He was so excited! He picked it up and showed it to his sister, Sydney.

Logan decided to make a special home for the caterpillar. With Sydney's help, they found an old glass jar and put an old piece of screen on top of it. They also placed leaves in it.

Next, Logan carefully lowered the caterpillar into its new home. It wiggled a lot, and this made Logan laugh.

Each day, Logan would check on his green furry friend and bring more leaves for it to eat. He was surprised at how much it ate and grew each day.

Logan also liked to play with his caterpillar. He made it walk up a stick and had fun counting the caterpillar's many legs.

One day, Logan noticed the caterpillar was hanging upside down from the screen on top of the jar. He tapped the glass jar to try to make it move, but the caterpillar didn't budge. He wondered if it was sleeping.

The next day, Logan and his family were going on vacation for a week, so he decided to check on his caterpillar before they left. It was still hanging upside down. He got a little worried but hoped it would be okay by the time he returned. He knew his caterpillar might get hungry while he was gone, so he added more leaves and a piece of apple to the jar.

When Logan returned home from his family's vacation, he quickly ran to see his caterpillar. He was so excited to see his green furry friend because he missed him so much.

To his amazement, there was a butterfly in its place! He called Sydney over to see the butterfly. The butterfly was beautiful. It had large yellow, black, and orange wings.

Logan wanted to keep the butterfly, but Sydney convinced him to set it free. She told him that it needed to fly and explore new things. At first, Logan was sad, but he knew his big sister was right. He slowly removed the screen top to set the butterfly free.

"Good-bye, butterfly! Good-bye!" said Logan with a big smile.

The End

Made in the USA
San Bernardino, CA
18 April 2016